小猪佩奇动画故事书第二辑

W9-AGA-607

乔治的新恐龙

英国快乐瓢虫出版公司　改编

圣孙鹏　译

 时代出版传媒股份有限公司
安徽少年儿童出版社

图书在版编目（CIP）数据

　　乔治的新恐龙 / 英国快乐瓢虫出版公司改编；圣孙鹏译 . 一合肥：
安徽少年儿童出版社，2016.5（2017.3 重印）
　　（小猪佩奇动画故事书第二辑）
　　ISBN 978-7-5397-8885-2

　　Ⅰ.①乔… Ⅱ.①英… ②圣… Ⅲ.①儿童文学 – 图画故事 – 英国 –
现代 Ⅳ.① I561.85

　　中国版本图书馆 CIP 数据核字（2016）第 081913 号

XIAOZHU PEIQI DONGHUA GUSHISHU DI'ERJI　　QIAOZHI DE XIN KONGLONG

小猪佩奇动画故事书第二辑·乔治的新恐龙

英国快乐瓢虫出版公司　改编
圣孙鹏　译

出 版 人：张克文	选题策划：李　琳	责任编辑：李　琳　黄　馨
责任校对：于　睿	版权运作：古宏霞	特约编辑：苗　辉
责任印制：田　航		

出版发行：时代出版传媒股份有限公司 http://www.press-mart.com
　　　　　安徽少年儿童出版社 E-mail：ahse1984@163.com
　　　　　新浪官方微博：http://weibo.com/ahsecbs
　　　　　腾讯官方微博：http://t.qq.com/anhuishaonianer（QQ：2202426653）
　　　　　（安徽省合肥市翡翠路 1118 号出版传媒广场　邮政编码：230071）
　　　　　市场营销部电话：（0551）63533532（办公室）　63533524（传真）
　　　　　（如发现印装质量问题，影响阅读，请与本社市场营销部联系调换）

印　　制：合肥精艺印刷有限公司
开　　本：889mm×1194mm　1/20　　印张：1.6
版　　次：2016 年 5 月第 1 版　　2017 年 3 月第 16 次印刷

ISBN 978-7-5397-8885-2　　　　　　　定价：120.00 元（全 10 册）

人物介绍

嘿，小朋友们，你们好！我是小猪佩奇。我来自英国，今年四岁了。我有一个可爱的弟弟，他叫乔治。我们和爸爸妈妈一起幸福地生活。我知道，在中国，我还有一个名字叫"粉红猪小妹"。这算是我的绰号吧。不过，悄悄地告诉你们：我还是更喜欢小朋友叫我的大名——小猪佩奇哟。

很多小朋友都看过我的动画片和故事书，并且很喜欢我和乔治。这可太让我高兴了！这一次，给大家带来了我和乔治的十个新故事。小朋友可以跟随我们一起去度假、滑雪、划船、在朋友家过夜……

还等什么，快来吧！

乔治最心爱的玩具
就是恐龙先生。

这天晚上睡觉前，
佩奇说："乔治，我想恐
龙先生的尾巴断了！"

3

"哇……"乔治哭了。

猪妈妈和猪爸爸跑过来
看看乔治为什么哭。

"可怜的乔治，"猪爸爸说，"也许是时候给你买个新恐龙了。"

第二天，佩奇、乔治、猪妈妈和猪爸爸一起来到狐狸先生的商店。

"看，乔治！"猪爸爸指着橱窗说，"这儿有一个大恐龙！"

"哦，恐——农（龙）！"乔治兴奋地说。

"早上好！"狐狸先生满脸笑容，"有什么需要效劳的？"

猪爸爸说："我们想买橱窗里那个恐龙。"

"好眼力！"狐狸先生说，"这是吼叫龙。它会走路，会说话，还会唱歌呢！"

"吼——叫——农（龙）！"乔治非常激动。

猪爸爸说："我们就买这个吧！"

花园里，乔治把吼叫龙抛起来接住，抛起来接住……

　　"小心点，乔治，"猪爸爸说，"别玩得太剧烈了，吼叫龙会摔坏的。"

洗澡的时候乔治想带着吼叫龙一起玩。

哗啦！
哗啦！

哗啦！

可是妈妈说："乔治，吼叫龙要是湿了就坏了。"

佩奇和乔治躺在床上睡得正香，忽然，吼叫龙启动了！

"嗷！吼叫龙，吼叫龙！"

"乔治！"佩奇说，"吼叫龙都把我吵醒啦！"

"或许吼叫龙应该换个地方睡觉。"猪爸爸说，他把吼叫龙拿走了。

乔治感到很难过。

他不能在花园里拿吼叫龙扔着玩，不能和它一起洗澡，甚至不能抱着它睡觉。

"没关系，乔治，"猪妈妈笑着安慰他，"吼叫龙还会吼叫啊。"

"吼叫龙！听我……吼……"吼叫龙彻底不动也不说话了。

猪妈妈说："我想一定是电池没电了。"

"没电啦？它需要几节电池呢？"猪爸爸嘟哝着把电池从吼叫龙肚子里倒出来。

佩奇一边捡电池一边叫道："太多啦！"

佩奇发现灌木丛下面有个绿色的东西："那是什么？"

"你找到了恐龙先生的尾巴，"猪妈妈说，"这下猪爸爸可以把它修好了。"

尾巴被很顺利地装回了原来的位置。

猪爸爸修好了恐龙先生。

"你好，恐龙先生。"佩奇说。

乔治回答："咯，咯，咯！"

在这个世界上，乔治最心爱的
玩具就是恐龙先生。

咔嗒！

第 2 页

George's favourite toy is Mr Dinosaur.
At bedtime Peppa says, "George, I think Mr Dinosaur is broken!"

第 4 页

"Waaaaaaah. . ." cries George.
Mummy and Daddy Pig come in to see why George is crying.

第 5 页

"Poor George," says Daddy Pig. "Maybe it's time you got a new dinosaur."

The next day, Peppa, George, Mummy and Daddy Pig visit Mr Fox's shop.

"Look, George!" says Daddy Pig pointing to the shop window. "There's a big one!"

"Oooh dine-saw!" says George.

"Good morning!" beams Mr Fox. "Can I help you?"

"We'd like to buy the dinosaur in the window, please," says Daddy Pig.

"Good choice!" says Mr Fox. "This is Dino-Roar. He walks, he talks and he sings!"

"Dino-ROAR!" says George excitedly.

"We'll take it!" says Daddy Pig.

George is playing with Dino-Roar in the garden. "Careful, George," says Daddy Pig. "Don't play too roughly because Dino-Roar will get broken."

George wants to play with Dino-Roar in the bath.
SPLASH!
SPLASH!
SPLASH!

But Mummy Pig says, "George, if you get Dino-Roar wet, he'll stop working."

第 14 页

Peppa and George are asleep in bed. But suddenly Dino-Roar comes to life!

"ROAR! Dino-Roar, Dino-Roar!"

"George!" says Peppa. "Dino-Roar has woken me up!"

"Maybe Dino-Roar should sleep somewhere else," says Daddy Pig, taking Dino-Roar away.

第 16 页

George is feeling sad.

He cannot play with Dino-Roar in the garden, or the bath or even in bed.

第 17 页

"Never mind, George," says Mummy Pig brightly. "Dino-Roar can still roar."

"Dino-Roar! Li . . . sten to Dino-Roo . . . aarr."

Dino-Roar stops walking and talking completely.

"I think the batteries must have run out," says Mummy Pig.

"Already? How many are there?" grumbles Daddy Pig, as batteries pour out of Dino-Roar. "Hundreds and thousands!" cries Peppa, as she picks them up.

Peppa spots something green under a bush. "What's this?" says Peppa.

"You've found Mr Dinosaur's tail," says Mummy Pig. "Now Daddy Pig can mend him."

第 22 页

The tail slips perfectly into place.
Daddy Pig has mended Mr Dinosaur.
"Hello, Mr Dinosaur," says Peppa.
"Grrrrr!" replies George.

第 23 页

Mr Dinosaur is George's favourite toy in the whole world.
CLICK!

快乐学英语

看完了这本故事书，让我们来学习几个与乔治的新恐龙相关的单词和句子吧。

dinosaur 恐龙

shop 商店

tail 尾巴

George´s favourite toy
is Mr Dinosaur.
乔治最心爱的玩具
就是恐龙先生。

George is feeling sad.
乔治感到很难过。